SPEAK UP!

Written by
Nathan Bryon

Illustrated by
Dapo Adeola

To Noah, Oscar, Finley, Athena, Orla — I can't wait to watch you
all grow up and Speak Up! (RIP BIG C — a real one, woof woof) — N.B.

To Joe, Monica, Chloe, Sallyanne and Nathan. Thanks for being the absolute
BEST team to work with. And to all our readers for showing us love.
#TeamRocketForLife — D.A.

PUFFIN BOOKS

UK | USA | Canada | Ireland | Australia | India | New Zealand | South Africa

Puffin Books is part of the Penguin Random House group of companies whose
addresses can be found at global.penguinrandomhouse.com.

Penguin
Random House
UK

First published 2023
001

Text copyright © Nathan Bryon, 2023
Illustrations copyright © Dapo Adeola, 2023

The moral right of the author and illustrator has been asserted

Billy and the Beast © 2018, cover reproduced with permission of Nadia Shireen
Billy and the Dragon © 2019, cover reproduced with permission of Nadia Shireen
Mabel and the Mountain © 2020, cover reproduced with permission of Kim Hillyard
How to be a Lion © 2018, cover reproduced with permission of Ed Vere
Barbara Throws a Wobbler © 2021, cover reproduced with permission of Nadia Shireen

Printed in Italy

The authorized representative in the EEA is Penguin Random House Ireland,
Morrison Chambers, 32 Nassau Street, Dublin D02 YH68

A CIP catalogue record for this book is available from the British Library

ISBN: 978–0–241–34587–0

All correspondence to: Puffin Books, Penguin Random House Children's
One Embassy Gardens, 8 Viaduct Gardens, London SW11 7BW

FSC
www.fsc.org

MIX
Paper from
responsible sources
FSC® C018179

Tomorrow is my favourite day of the week.
IT'S NEW BOOK DAY!

Every Friday after school, Mum, Jamal
(he's my big brother) and I go to the library
to borrow our new books for the week.

DID YOU KNOW
there are over 2 million
new books published
every year!

I read more books than anyone else in my family.
I used to find reading difficult but the more I do
it, the better I get.

Jamal says I eat books for breakfast, lunch and dinner,
but the thought of eating books is gross!

Eurgh

Jamal says he likes books about history,
but we only ever see him reading
books about romance.

I **LOVE** all kinds of books . . .

books that teach me unbelievable facts,

books that take me on adventures,

and books about great people who changed the world.

I've just been reading all about Rosa Parks.

DID YOU KNOW

Rosa Parks led a famous protest? She had been told to give up her seat on the bus to a white man – just because of the colour of her skin – and she said **NO!**

The library is in a **HUGE** building that used to be a theatre. It's a bit old and dusty, but I love it.

There are books
EVERYWHERE!

The library is mainly for quiet reading,
but sometimes authors and illustrators come to
read stories – and then it can get quite **NOISY!**

Today, Layla the librarian hands me a book she thinks I'll love. She always has the best recommendations.

She also gives me a party invitation!

I LOVE PARTIES!

But Layla says it's a **GOODBYE** party. There isn't enough money to keep the library open, so it has to close down.

OH NO!

The next day, everybody goes to the library-closing party. But it doesn't feel like a party.

There is food —
but **no-one's** eating.

There are books – but no one's reading.

Everyone just looks . . . **sad.**
Nobody wants the
library to close.

There must be
something we can do!

On Monday at school, I start **SPEAKING UP** about libraries and how brilliant they are.

DID YOU KNOW there have been libraries for over 5,000 years!

DID YOU KNOW
one overdue library book was returned after 288 years!

DID YOU KNOW
there's a library in Portugal with a family of bats that eat the book-damaging bugs?

By the end of the day, everyone in my class
wants to stop the library from closing too.

But what do we do? What can we do?

We need to **SPEAK UP!** But how?

I've got it!

We'll have a peaceful protest – like Rosa Parks did!

We work together to get prepared and spread the word.
Our teachers, our parents and Layla the librarian all help.

And by the weekend, we're ready to go!

SAVE OUR LIBRARY!

Lots of people join our peaceful protest outside the library.

They're all wearing my favourite outfit – we **look** amazing.
We're so loud we can probably be heard from the Moon!
With everyone **SPEAKING UP** together, surely someone will listen.

After the peaceful protest there
is good news and bad news.

The good news is that everyone is talking about our protest —
it's even on the TV and the internet.

The bad news is that day after day after day . . .
nothing has changed. The library is still closing.

What was the point?

But one day the post comes.
No one ever sends me letters!

And it's not just one or two — there are hundreds.

They're from people who saw the peaceful protest –
and they're amazing . . .

Dear Rocket,

I saw your protest from my bedroom window the other day, and I was super inspired by how you got everyone in the community to care about the library. The library is one of my favourite places in the whole world and I want to help you save it!

Noah

While I'm reading the letters, the doorbell rings . . .

And it's the mayor of our whole town!

She explains that people around the world were
inspired by our protest – and lots of them have
given money to help save the library.

She thanks me for **SPEAKING UP** and
gives me an invitation to a celebration.

This sounds like a party I definitely want to go to!

The library celebration is **AWESOME!**
The mayor tells us that enough money was raised
to refurbish the library and buy lots of new books.

There's food – and **everyone's eating!**

There are books – and **everyone's reading!**

Suddenly we hear a loud **beeeeeeeep!** What's that?

It's Layla the librarian with a **HUGE** bus!